CHILDREN'S CLASSICS

Treasure Island

By
Robert Louis Stevenson

Adapted by
Mary Kerr

Edited by
Sophie Evans

Published by BK Books Ltd
First published in 2007
Copyright © BK Books Ltd

ISBN: 978-1-906068-48-6
Printed in China

Contents

Chapter 1

The Mysterious Captain at the Admiral Benbow

I, Jim Hawkins, am putting down this story of the Treasure Island on record, as wished by Squire Trelawney, Doctor Livesey, and the remaining crew members, because of the uniqueness of the mission involved.

I was just a young boy then, living in Black Hill Cove. My father ran an inn called the Admiral Benbow. It was a popular inn, as guests were well looked after. Moreover, being away from the villages, it provided the

1

required privacy and peace to the travelers. One day, a tall, strong-looking man came to our inn. He wore a soiled, patchy blue coat and walked rather heavily. His hands were ragged and scarred with black broken nails and across one of his cheeks he had a deep white cut. A man followed him with a heavy sea-chest, in a wheelbarrow.

Looking all around the place and whistling to himself, the tall man broke out in that old sea-song in a deep, shaky voice, a song which was frequently heard afterwards;

"Fifteen men on the dead man's chest,
Yo-ho-ho and a bottle of rum!"

"This looks like a comfortable place," he said.

"Here, you, buddy!" he cried to the man who pushed the barrow. "Bring up my chest. I'll stay here for some time."

"I'll stay here for a while," he then told my father. "Call me 'Captain'. I am a simple man. All I want is rum, bacon, eggs, and a

room upstairs so that I can watch the ships at sea. Oh, I see what you are about to say—here." He threw down three or four gold pieces on my father's desk. "You can tell me when I have exhausted that," he said, fiercely.

Despite his filthy clothes, he did not seem like a man who merely worked on a ship, but more like a commander, who was accustomed to be obeyed or to strike! The man who came with the barrow, told us that Captain had inquired about all the inns along the coast, but had chosen ours for the privacy, peace and quiet that it offered.

That was all we could learn of our overbearing and mysterious new guest!

A reserved man by nature, Captain loitered around every day and sat on the hills with a brass telescope, scrutinizing the vast expanse of the sea. He spent his evenings sitting in a corner of the parlor, next to the fire, drinking rum. After coming back from his stroll, he would ask me if I had seen any sailors walking along by the inn. At first I thought he was only looking for another seaman who could give him company, but later I realized that he actually wanted to avoid them.

Whenever a seaman came to stay at our inn, Captain would look at him through the curtained door before entering the parlor. Strangely, he always remained as silent as a mouse in front of sailors. One day, Captain took me aside and promised me a silver four-penny on the first of every month, if I would only watch out for a sailor with one leg and immediately inform him. I now shared his secret!

Often, at the beginning of the month, when I would ask Captain for my silver four-penny, he would only blow through his nose and stare down at me. But, before the end of the week, he would, inevitably, bring me my money and repeat his orders to look out for the 'one-legged seafarer'.

Oh! How the image of this creature with one leg haunted me!

I would see him in various diabolical forms, with one leg cut off at the knee and then at the hip. The thoughts of this monstrous creature kept me awake on dark

stormy nights, when the waves roared and hit high on the cliffs.

Although I was terrified by the idea of the sailor with one leg, I was not much scared of Captain.

On nights, when he was more drunk than usual, he would sit at his table singing his wild sea-songs. Then he insisted the people present in the inn were to join him and listen to his frightening stories, stories about hanging, walking the plank and wild storms at sea, etc. Dreadful indeed!

It seemed by his own account that Captain must have lived his life among some of the wickedest men upon the sea. The filthy language in which he told these stories shocked the simple country people.

My father always said that the inn would be ruined, for people would soon stop coming, for fear of facing Captain and his weird behavior. But I believed that his presence benefited us. Although frightened, people rather liked it, as it provided some excitement in their quiet, country life. There was even a group of young men who pretended to admire him and called him a 'true sea-dog' and a 'real old salt'.

However, Captain did, in a way, cause our ruin. He continued staying with us for weeks at a time and soon, the money he had paid to my father on his arrival was exhausted. Still, my father could not gather courage to ask him for more money. If ever he mentioned it, Captain blew through his nose so loudly that it scared my poor father out of the room. I firmly believe that this was the sole cause of the untimely death of my father.

During his stay at our inn, Captain never changed his clothes. I remember the appearance of his coat, it was full of patches. He never wrote or received any letters, and he never spoke with anyone, except the visitors of our inn, and that, too, only when he was drunk. I saw Captain lose his temper only once. At that time my father was seriously ill and Doctor Livesey had come to see him. After examining him, the doctor sat in our parlor talking to old Taylor, the gardener, when suddenly Captain began to sing his favorite song,

"Fifteen men on the dead man's chest,
Yo-ho-ho and a bottle of rum!
Drink and the devil had done for the
rest,
Yo-ho-ho and a bottle of rum!"

Doctor Livesey didn't like his singing so loudly, so he looked up angrily for a moment and continued talking to the gardener. In the meantime, Captain gradually brightened up at his own music and slapped his hand upon the table before him, in a way which all of us knew meant that we were expected to be silent.

The voices stopped at once, but Dr. Livesey's went on as before, speaking clearly and recurrently blowing at his pipe.

Captain glared at him for a while, slapped his hand again, glared still harder, and at last shouted with a sinful oath, "Silence there, between you two!"

"Were you addressing me, sir?" asked the doctor.

Captain replied, with another evil oath, that it was indeed so.

"I only want to say one thing, sir," replied the doctor, quietly. "If you keep on drinking rum, the world will soon be free of a very dirty miscreant!"

Enraged, Captain sprang to his feet. He drew a sailor's clasp knife, opened it, and threatened to pin the doctor to the wall.

The doctor remained unperturbed. He spoke calmly and steadily, in a voice that could be heard by all in the room. "If you do not put that knife this instant in your pocket, I promise, upon my honor, that you shall be hanged at the next hearing."

A battle of glares ensued between them, but Captain soon gave in and put down his weapon. He resumed his seat, grumbling to himself.

"And now, sir," continued the doctor, "since I know there is such a person as you in my district, I'll have an eye upon you day and night. I am not only a doctor, but a magistrate too. So, make sure I don't get even a single complaint against you."

Soon after, Doctor Livesey rode away. The Captain maintained his peace that evening and for many more evenings to come!

Chapter 2

The Terror of the
Black Dog

t was not very long after this
that there occurred the first
of the mysterious events that
finally freed us of Captain,
though not of his affairs.

It was a bitter, cold January morning,
with grey frosts and a mellowed sun. It
was clear to us that my poor father was
unlikely to survive till spring. He sank
day by day. My mother and I had to look
after the inn all by ourselves, without

paying much regard to our unpleasant guest.

One day, Captain rose earlier than usual and set out for the beach, his sword swinging under the broad skirts of the old blue coat and his brass telescope under his arm.

My mother was upstairs with father and I was laying the breakfast table, when the parlor door opened and a pale-looking man, with two fingers of his left hand missing, stepped in. Always on a lookout for the sailor with one leg, this one puzzled me. He did not resemble a sailor, and yet he had a touch of the sea about him. He sat down and called out to me.

"Come here, son," he said. "Come near."

I took a step nearer.

"Is this table for my friend, Bill?" he asked, sneeringly.

I told him this was for a person who stayed in our house, and whom we called Captain.

"Well," he said, "Bill can call himself Captain or by any other name that he pleases. Does your Captain have a cut on one cheek?"

"Yes," I replied.

"See? I told you that I know Captain. Now, where is he?"

14

"Well, he has gone out for a walk."

"Ah! I'll tell you what, dear; you and I will just go into the parlor and hide behind the door. Then, we'll give Bill a little surprise when he walks in."

The expression on his face was not at all pleasant when he said this.

The stranger put me behind him in the corner, so that we were hidden from the open door. I was very frightened, and it rather added to my fears to observe that the stranger was frightened himself. All the time, while we were waiting, he kept swallowing as if he felt a lump in his throat.

We kept waiting behind the inn door, looking closely round the corner like a cat waiting for a mouse. At last, Captain walked in. He slammed the door behind him and sat down at the breakfast table.

"Bill," said the stranger, in a voice which I thought he had tried to make bold and big.

Captain turned around. His face went pale, as if he had seen a ghost. I felt sorry to see him look so old and sick in a moment.

"Come on, Bill, surely you recognize me," said the stranger.

Captain gasped. "Black Dog!" he whispered.

"And who else?" replied the other, with a smirk. "Black Dog, who has come to see his old shipmate, Billy. Let us both have some rum, and sit and talk like old shipmates."

The stranger then asked me to bring two glasses of rum. I left them together and went into the bar. When I returned with the rum, they were already seated on either side of Captain's breakfast table.

Black Dog instructed me to go out of the room and leave the door wide open. For a long time I heard nothing but their murmuring. Once, I heard Captain cry out, "No, no, no, no!"

All of a sudden, there was a loud noise of chairs and tables crashing. This was followed by the sound of clashing steel and then there was a cry of pain. The next moment the door opened, and I saw Black Dog running and Captain hotly pursuing, both with drawn swords. Black Dog had a big cut on his left shoulder, which was bleeding profusely.

Once out on the road, Black Dog disappeared over the edge of the hill in half a minute.

Captain returned to the inn and cried out, "Jim! I must get away from here. Rum! Rum!" And as he said this, he stumbled and caught himself with one hand against the wall.

"Are you hurt?" cried I.

"Rum," he repeated.

I rushed to get it. As I was coming back with the glass of rum, I heard a loud thud in the parlor. Rushing in, I found Captain lying unconscious on the floor. At the same moment, my mother, alarmed by the cries, came running downstairs to help me. Both of us tried to raise Captain's head. He was breathing very loud and hard, but his eyes were closed and his face had turned deathly pale.

"Dear me!" cried my mother. "Is he dead?"

Not knowing where he was hurt, I felt helpless. I got the rum and tried to pour it down his throat, but his teeth were tightly clenched and his jaw as strong as iron. At that moment the door opened and Doctor Livesey, who had come in to see my father, entered.

"Oh, doctor!" we cried out together. "What shall we do? Where is he wounded?"

"Wounded!" exclaimed the doctor, after taking a look at Captain. "He is not wounded. He has had a stroke."

The doctor asked my mother to go upstairs to my father, and told me to fetch a bowl. Then he ripped Captain's sleeve and exposed his arm to take out some blood. We saw that Captain's arm was tattooed in several places. 'Here's luck', 'A fair wind', and 'Billy Bones his fancy', were very neatly and clearly executed on his forearm, and up near the shoulder there was a sketch of a gallows and a man hanging from it.

We figured out from these tattoos that Captain's real name was Billy Bones.

The doctor then took his scalpel and opened a vein in Captain's arm. Once he had drawn out a lot of blood, Captain mistily opened his eyes and looked about him. Then, the two of us managed to take him to his bed upstairs.

"Drinking rum will be the cause of his death," said the doctor, as soon as he had closed the door. "I have drawn enough blood to keep him quiet for some time. He should lie for a week, where he is. But, he will not survive another attack."

Chapter 3

The Warning of the Black Spot

he next day, around noon, I went to Captain's room with some cool drinks and medicines. He lay awake in bed, seemingly weak but excited.

"Jim," he said, "you're the only one who's worth anything, and you know I've always been good to you. You'll bring me a glass of rum, won't you?"

I told him that the doctor had said he was to lie in bed for at least a week.

On hearing this, Captain became very excited.

"A WEEK!" he cried. "I can't do that. They'd have the Black Spot on me by then."

As he spoke, he rose from the bed, with great difficulty, clutching at my shoulder with a grip that almost made me cry out. Finally, he sat on the edge and murmured, "That doctor's finished me. My ears are ringing. Lay me back."

Before I could do much to help him, Captain had fallen back again to his former place, where he lay silent for a while.

"Jim," he said, after a moment, "that seaman, Black Dog, was a bad one, but the people who have sent him after me are even worse. If they give me the Black Spot, then run to the doctor and tell him to gather as many people as he can, and bring them to the inn. Mind you, it's my old sea-chest they are after. I was Flint's first companion, Jim,

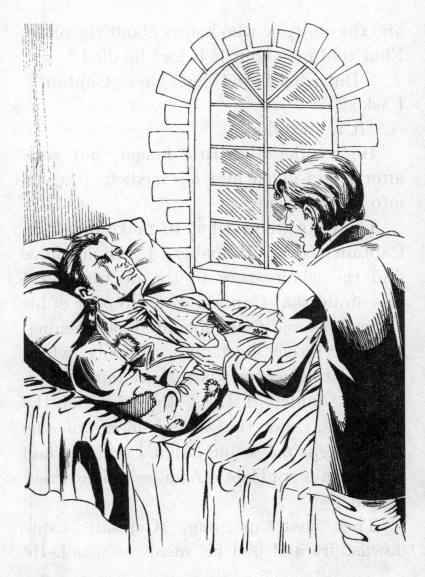

and the only one who knows about the place. Flint told me about it before he died."

"But what is the Black Spot, Captain?" I asked.

"It is an order."

He wondered a little longer, but soon after I had given him his medicine, he fell into a deep sleep.

I did not know what to make out from Captain's talk. Probably, I should have told the whole story to the doctor, but I was afraid that Captain would repent of his confessions and finish me off. That evening, my poor father died quite suddenly, which put all other matters out of my mind.

Our sudden distress, the visits of the neighbors, and the arrangement of the funeral kept me so busy that I scarcely had time to think of Captain, far less to be afraid of him.

The next morning, Captain came downstairs and had his meals as usual. He ate little and had more than his usual supply of rum.

On the night before my father's funeral, he was drunk as ever and sang his ugly old sea-song loudly. Although shocking in a house of mourning, no one dared to stop him. He was so weak that we all feared his death. The doctor had to leave suddenly to attend a case many miles away, and so was unavailable after my father's death.

Instead of recovering, Captain seemed to grow weaker. He climbed up and down the stairs, and went from the parlor to the bar and back again. At times, he would put his nose out of doors to smell the sea, holding onto the walls for support and breathing hard and fast, like a man on a steep mountain.

So, things went on until the day after the funeral. It was about three o'clock in the afternoon. I was standing at the door, sadly remembering my father, when I saw someone walking slowly along the road. He was blind, for he carried a stick with him, which he tapped on the ground as he walked. He wore a green shade over his eyes, was hunched, and wore a tattered old sea cloak with a hood. I never saw, in my life, a more dreadful looking person. He stopped a little distance from our inn and cried, "Will any kind friend inform a poor blind man, where, or in which part of this country he may now be ?"

"You are at the Admiral Benbow, Black Hill Cove," I said.

"I hear a young voice," said he. "Will you give me your hand, my kind, young friend, and take me in?"

I held out my hand, and he gripped it immediately like a clamp. Taken aback, I struggled to withdraw, but the blind man pulled me close with a jerk of his arm.

"Now, boy," he said, "take me in to Captain."

The horrible, soft-spoken, eyeless creature twisted my arm as he spoke, which made me cry out in pain.

I obeyed him at once, and walked straight towards the parlor.

"Lead me straight up to him!" commanded the blind man. "And when I am in view, cry out, 'Here's a friend for you, Bill'!"

I did as I was instructed, and cried out the words in a trembling voice.

The poor Captain, who was drinking rum, raised his eyes. One look at the man, and the entire color drained out of him.

"Now, Bill, sit where you are!" said the blind man. "I can't see, but I can hear if a finger is moving. Now, you boy, take his left hand by the wrist and bring it near to my right."

I obeyed the blind man, and saw him pass something from his hand into the palm of Captain. Captain instantly closed his palm.

"And now that's done," said the blind man. Saying this, he suddenly let hold of me and walked out of the parlor without any difficulty. I stood still as I heard his stick go tap-tap-tapping into the distance.

It was quite some time before either Captain or I could gather our senses. Captain slowly opened his palm and cried out, "Ten o'clock! Six hours. I will escape them!" And he sprang to his feet.

As he did so, he put his hand to his throat, stood swaying for a moment, and finally, with a strange cry, fell on his face upon the floor.

I ran to him at once, calling my mother. But all haste was in vain. Captain was dead. The second stroke had killed him!

Although I had never liked the man, I burst into a flood of tears. It was the second death I had known, and the sorrow of the first was still fresh in my heart.

Chapter 4

The Key to the Sea-Chest

ithout losing time, I told my mother all that I knew about Captain. I regretted that I had not told her all this before. I made her understand that it was quite dangerous to be here.

Even though Captain owed us some money, we didn't suppose Black Dog, the blind man, and his friends would let us take Captain's possessions. I told my mother of Captain's order to run to the doctor

29

immediately and call for help. But if I did so, my mother would be left alone. And I did not want to take that risk.

Scared and lonely, we decided that we should go to the nearby village for help, and accordingly, we ran out at once in the frosty fog.

It was already evening when we reached the village. We told the villagers of our troubles and begged them for help, but no one agreed to return with us to the Admiral Benbow. The name of Captain Flint (the captain of the pirates) was well-known to some of the people there, and carried a great deal of terror.

After everyone had declined to go, my mother made the villagers a speech. She declared angrily that she would not lose the money that belonged to her fatherless boy.

"If none of you dare," she said, "Jim and I dare. We will go and take the money."

The villagers were shocked at my mother's decision, but even then nobody accompanied

us. They merely handed me a loaded pistol in case we were attacked, and told us that one fellow would ride forward to the doctor's house in search of armed assistance.

My heart was thumping with fear as my mother and I set forth in the cold night upon our dangerous venture. We slipped along the hedges, swiftly and noiselessly, till, to our relief, the door of the Admiral Benbow had closed behind us.

I bolted the door carefully. We stood and caught our breath for a moment in the dark. We were alone in the house with the dead body of Captain. My mother got a candle, and then, holding each other's hands, we went into the parlor.

Captain lay as we had left him, on his back, with his eyes open and one arm stretched out.

"Draw the curtains, Jim," whispered my mother. "Someone might be watching us. We now have to get the key from his body."

I went down on my knees at once. On the floor, close to Captain's hand, there was a little round of paper, blackened on one side. I was sure that this was the Black Spot. On the other side of the paper was written: 'YOU HAVE TILL TEN TONIGHT'.

"Mother, look, this says he had time till ten. That means they won't come back till ten. We have a lot of time."

At this very moment, our old clock began to strike, startling and shocking us. However, we were relieved to know that it was only six.

"Now, Jim," my mother said, "the key."

I felt in Captain's pockets, one after another, but all I found was some coins, some thread and big needles, a bit of tobacco, a knife, a pocket compass, and a tinderbox.

"Perhaps, it's round his neck," suggested my mother.

Overcoming a strong aversion, I tore open Captain's shirt at the neck. Sure enough, hanging to a bit of string, was the KEY! I cut the string, took the key, and hurried upstairs to the little room where Captain's chest had stood since the day of his arrival.

"Give me the key," said my mother. Although the lock was very stiff, she opened it in a twinkling.

A strong smell of tobacco rose from the chest, but nothing was to be seen on the top except a suit of very good cloth. Beneath that we found a couple of pistols, a piece of silver bar, an old watch, a compass and some other trinkets. Beneath all this, at the bottom of the chest, was a bundle tied up in oilcloth and a purse of gold coins.

"I'll show these rogues that I am an honest woman," said my mother. "I'll have my dues, and not a penny more."

Then, she began to count out the amount of money which Captain owed us during his long stay. It was a long and difficult business, for the coins were from all countries and sizes, mixed up randomly.

When we were about halfway through, I heard, in the silent frosty air, the tap, tapping of the blind man's stick upon the frozen road! My heart skipped a beat! The sound drew nearer and nearer and then there was a sharp knock at the door. Then, we heard the handle being turned and the bolt rattling, as someone tried to enter.

I held my mother's hand and both of us sat quietly for a long time. Finally, to our great relief and joy, the knocking stopped and we could hear the blind man walking away.

Mother resumed her counting.

Suddenly, a low whistle sounded at a distance. It seemed that the pirates were signaling each other.

"I'll take what I have," my mother said, jumping to her feet.

"And I'll take this," said I, picking up the oilskin packet.

The next moment, we opened the door and were in full retreat. The fog was rapidly dispersing and the moon shone quite clear. At a distance, I heard the sound of several footsteps and as we looked back in their direction, we saw that one of them carried a lantern.

"My dear," said my mother, suddenly, "take the money and run on. I am going to faint."

'This is certainly the end for both of us,' I thought.

We were just near a little bridge, so I helped my mother down the bank. There, she gave a little sigh and fainted. I somehow dragged her a little way under the arch. I could not move her any further. So, we had to stay there, my mother almost entirely exposed, and both of us within earshot of the inn. I could hear all that happened in the inn.

Chapter 5

The Missing Packet

My curiosity took over my fear, and I crept back to the bank so that I could observe the road and the inn door. As I positioned myself, my enemies, seven or eight of them, began to arrive. Three men ran together, hand in hand. I recognized the man in the middle to be the blind man.

"Break the door!" he cried.

The men obeyed, but were taken aback to find the door already open. The blind man shouted once again, impatiently, "In, in!"

The men barged into the house, and for a moment everything seemed still. Then one of them uttered a cry of surprise and a voice screamed, "Bill's dead!"

"Search him, one of you, and the rest go up and get the chest!" cried the blind man.

I could hear the rattling of feet up our old wooden stairs. Then one of them threw open the window of Captain's room. A man leaned out into the moonlight and addressed the blind man on the road below.

"Pew," he cried, "someone has searched the chest!"

"Is it there?" roared Pew.

"The money is there!"

"Curse the money! Is Flint's packet there?"

"We can't find it anywhere!" was the reply. "Someone has taken it!"

"I know who has done it!" screamed the blind man. "It is that boy, the innkeeper's son! Find him!"

Immediately, the men started ransacking our inn. The doors were kicked in and the furniture overthrown. Suddenly, we heard a whistle. It was a signal for the seamen.

"That's Dirk's signal," said one of them. "We must move now."

But Pew did not want to give up on the search.

"Move!" cried he. "Why, they must be somewhere close by! Scatter and look for them!"

"They must have hidden that precious thing," answered one. "There is no reason for you to stand and scream. We are not going to find it anyway."

As soon as Pew heard this, he went mad with rage. He struck at the pirates, right and left. Soon, a violent quarrel ensued. While the quarrel was still raging, another sound came from the top of the hill, at the side of the village. It was the tramp of galloping horses. The pirates turned at once and ran, so that in half a minute not a sign of them remained but Pew.

Pew remained behind, tapping up and down the road in frenzy. He kept calling out for his comrades. "Johnny, Black Dog, Dirk, you won't leave old Pew like that, not old Pew!"

Just then, the noise of horses became louder, and four or five riders came in sight in the moonlight and swept at full gallop

down the slope. Pew turned with a scream, and ran right under the hoofs of the nearest horse. The rider tried to save him, but in vain.

Down went Pew with a loud cry.

I leaped to my feet and greeted the riders. They were stopping anyways because of the accident. One of them was the boy who had gone to Dr. Livesey's to get help, and the rest were officers he had met on the way.

Pew was dead, stone dead. As for my mother, she was carried up to the village. A little cold water and salts soon revived her.

I went back with the supervisor, Mr. Dance, to the Admiral Benbow Inn, which had been ransacked and almost destroyed by Pew's men. Although nothing had actually been taken away except Captain's moneybag and a little silver, I could see at once that we were ruined. Mr. Dance could make nothing of the scene. But I realized that the paper I had kept in my pocket was very valuable.

Chapter 6

Clues to the Treasure

 knew that the only man who could help me was Doctor Livesey. As Mr. Dance was riding to the doctor's house to inform him of the incident, I requested him to take me with him. Mr. Dance readily agreed to this, and we rode speedily till we reached Dr. Livesey's house. However, a housemaid informed us that the doctor was dining at Squire Trelawney's place, and so we headed for the squire's house. On reaching there, we were taken to a great library where the squire and Doctor Livesey sat smoking pipes, sitting on either side of the fire.

The squire was a tall man, over six feet high and broadly built. He had a rough face with very black eyebrows that moved readily and this gave him a look of short temper.

"Come in, Mr. Dance," he said, majestically.

"Good evening, Dance," said the doctor, with a nod. "And good evening to you, friend Jim. What good purpose brings you here?"

Mr. Dance told his story like a lesson. The two gentlemen leaned forward with a lot of interest and even forgot to smoke. When they heard that my mother had gone back to the inn, the squire cried out, "Bravo!"

When Mr. Dance finished the story, he was much complimented by both the doctor and the squire. After some time, he took his leave and went away.

"And so, Jim," said the doctor, turning to me, "do you have the thing that the pirates were after?"

"Here it is, sir," I said, and gave him the oilskin packet.

"You have heard of this Flint, I suppose?" the doctor asked the squire.

"Heard of him!" cried the squire. "Heard of him, you say! He was the most murderous pirate who ever sailed."

"Well, I've heard of him myself in England," said the doctor, gravely. "But the point is, did he have money?"

"Money!" cried the squire. "What do you think these villains were after?"

"That we shall soon know," replied the doctor. "Now, with Jim's approval we'll open the packet." Saying this, he laid the packet on the table. The bundle contained two things, a book and a sealed paper.

"First of all we'll try the book," said the doctor.

The squire and I both peered over his shoulder as he opened it. On the first page there were only some scraps of writing and the next ten or twelve pages were filled with a curious series of entries.

"This looks like the villain's account book!" cried the squire. "Now, let us see the other."

The paper had been sealed in several places with a metal ring. The doctor opened the seals with great care, and there fell out the map of an island, with latitude and longitude, and every particular that would be needed to bring a ship safely to the shores. It was about nine miles long and five across and had two fine land-locked harbors, and a hill in the center marked 'The Spyglass'. There were three crosses of red ink, two on the north part of the island and one in the southwest, and beside this, in the same red ink, was written 'BULK OF TREASURE HERE'.

On the back of the map, this information had been written further:

TALL TREE,

SPYGLASS SHOULDER, BEARING A POINT TO THE N. OF N.N.E. SKELETON ISLAND E.S.E. AND BY E. TEN FEET.

Although I was not able to make much out of the map, the doctor and the squire were filled with delight.

"Livesey," said the squire, "you shall give up your practice at once! I will arrange for the best ship in a week's time, and we will set out in hunt of the treasure. Hawkins shall come as the cabin boy, and you shall be the ship's doctor. I'll be

the admiral. We'll take Redruth, Joyce, and Hunter. We'll set sail and will surely be able to find the island without much difficulty."

"Trelawney," said the doctor, "I'll go with you; so will Jim. But there is one man I am afraid of."

"And who's that?" cried the squire. "Name the dog, sir!"

"You," replied the doctor, "for you cannot hold your tongue. We are not the only men who know of this paper. These fellows, who had attacked the inn tonight, know about it too and are obviously after that treasure. Not one of us must breathe a word of what we've found."

"Livesey," replied the squire, "you are always right. I'll be as silent as the grave."

It took us longer than what the squire had said to leave for the island. The doctor had to go to London to arrange for a physician to take charge of his practice, and the squire to Bristol. In the meanwhile, I lived on at the squire's place under the charge of old Redruth, the gamekeeper.

Several weeks passed by and then, one day, we received a letter from the squire. The letter was addressed to the doctor, but with this addition: 'To be opened, in the case of his absence, by Tom Redruth or young Hawkins'.

Obeying this order, we opened the letter and found the following important news:

Old Anchor Inn, Bristol, March 1st.

Dear Livesey,

The ship has been bought and fitted. She lies at anchor, ready to set sail. She is called 'the Hispaniola'. I got her through my old friend, Blandly. You would be happy to know that I have already appointed a man named Long John Silver, who has lost a leg in his country's service, as the ship's cook. I met him accidentally on the port. So now, Livesey, come here as soon as possible, and let young Hawkins go at once to see his mother, before he leaves for Bristol.

John Trelawney.

The letter filled Redruth and me with excitement. The next morning both of us set out for the Admiral Benbow and I was happy to find my mother in good health and spirits. The inn was all repaired, and the squire had added some furniture and gifted a beautiful armchair for my mother. A young boy had been appointed to help my mother in my absence.

The next day, after dinner, Redruth and I started for our journey. I said goodbye to my mother and the place where I had lived since I was born. I knew it would be a long time before I came back to the dear old Admiral Benbow. The mail van picked us up at the Royal George. After some time I fell asleep, and when I woke up, it was quite late in the morning. There were tall buildings all around us.

"Where are we?" I asked.

"Bristol," replied Tom. "Get down."

Mr. Trelawney was staying at an inn on the docks. As we walked down towards the inn, to my great delight, I saw a great number of ships of all sizes and of different nations. In one, sailors were singing at their work, in another, there were men overhead, hanging onto the ropes.

As we approached the squire's inn, we found him all dressed up like a sea-officer. He was coming out of the inn door with a smile on his face and walking like a sailor.

"Here you are!" he cried in excitement. "And the doctor came last night from London. Bravo! The ship's company is complete!"

"Oh, sir," I cried, "when do we sail?"

"SAIL! We sail tomorrow!"

Chapter 7

Chapter 7

Black Dog Again

fter I had my breakfast, the squire gave me a note addressed to Long John Silver. He told me that I would find him in a hotel with the signboard of a large brass telescope. It was called the 'Spyglass'.

I set off, overjoyed at this opportunity to see some more of the ships and seamen. I picked my way among a great crowd of people and carts, until I found the place I was looking for.

The hotel had a bright look. The sign was newly painted, the windows had neat red curtains and the floor was clean. The customers were mostly seafaring men and they talked so loudly that I stood at the door, almost afraid to enter.

As I was waiting, I saw a man, whose left leg was cut off, coming out of a side room. I was at once sure that he must be Long John Silver. He was very tall and strong, and had a big, pale, smiling face. He carried a crutch under his left shoulder, hopping about like a bird.

Now, to tell you the truth, since the doctor had mentioned it in his letter, I was afraid that the cook would be the same one-legged man that Captain had once asked me to watch out for. But one look at the man, and all my fears were dispelled. I had seen Captain, Black Dog, and the blind man, Pew, and I knew what a pirate was like. But this man was entirely different. He was clean and had a pleasant disposition.

Gathering up courage, I walked up to the man.

"Mr. Silver, sir?" I asked, holding out the note.

"Yes, my boy," he said. "That is my name. And who are you?"

As he said this, he looked at the letter I was holding out. Immediately, he exclaimed loudly, "Oh! So you are our new cabin boy. I am very pleased to see you." Saying so, he firmly grasped my hand.

Just then, one of the customers at the far side of the tavern rose abruptly and rushed towards the door. One glance at him, and I recognized him to be the man with two fingers missing, who had come to the Admiral Benbow.

"Stop him! It's Black Dog!" I shouted.

Silver looked in the direction I pointed and cried, "Harry, run and catch him. He is running away without paying us."

A man who was sitting near the door rushed after him, but Black Dog turned out to be faster than him. He returned after a while and reported that Black Dog had escaped.

Silver then turned to me and asked, "Who did you say he was? Black what?"

"Dog, sir," I said. "He is a pirate!"

"A pirate in my house!" cried Silver. "I have to report it to the doctor. Let's go!"

So we set out together to meet the squire and tell him about what had happened. As we walked along the port, Silver told me about the different ships that we passed by. He showed me how cargo from one ship was unloaded and loaded. Brimming with excitement, I found Long John Silver to be a nice friendly man and realized that he was one of the best possible shipmates one could have.

When we reached the inn, the squire and Doctor Livesey were about to leave for the ship. Long John told the story about the escaped pirate from beginning to end without lying or hiding anything. The two gentlemen were shocked to hear all this and regretted that Black Dog got away, but at the same time agreed that nothing could be done.

John Silver left after this, and I went with the squire and the doctor to see the ship.

As we stepped aboard the Hispaniola, we were met and greeted by the first mate, Mr. Arrow, a brown, old sailor with earrings in his ears and a squint. I saw that the squire and Mr. Arrow were very friendly. They showed me around the ship

and once we were inside the cabin, Mr. Arrow said the captain would like to meet them.

"Please show him in," said the squire.

The captain, who was close behind, entered at once and shut the door behind him. He was a sharp-looking man.

"Well, Captain Smollett, what have you to say?"

"Sir, I was asked to sail this ship as per this gentleman's directions, but now I believe that all the crew know more about the voyage than I do," the captain said. "That is not fair, is it? I have heard that we are sailing in hunt of treasure, which I do not like. And also that you even have a map with crosses marking out where the treasure is."

At this, the doctor and the squire exchanged surprised looks.

"I never told that to a soul!" cried the squire.

"All of them know it, sir," said the captain. "I don't like treasure voyages, and

I am not in favor of this voyage because it is supposed to be a secret one; but a secret that is no more a secret, that even a parrot knows!"

"Silver's parrot?" asked the squire.

"Do not worry, captain, we will handle it all," assured the doctor.

"I hope so, sir, because I hold myself responsible for the lives of the people aboard the ship," said the captain.

"You also say that you don't like the crew," said the doctor. "Are they not good seamen?"

"I don't like them, sir," returned Captain Smollett, "although I believe Mr. Arrow is a good seaman, but he's too free with the crew to be a good officer. A mate shouldn't drink with the men before the mast!"

"Captain," said the doctor, "tell us what you want."

"Well, gentlemen, are you determined to go on this cruise?"

"Like iron," answered the squire.

"Well then, I have a few suggestions to make: first, to give the few men whom you can trust, a berth here in the cabin; second, to put the powder and the arms under the cabin; and last, I don't know who has this map, but I ask you to keep it secret even from Mr. Arrow and me. Otherwise, I would request you to let me resign." Saying this, the captain left the cabin.

What the captain suggested sounded sensible and the doctor heartily approved of the captain's plan. The squire, too, agreed to go ahead with the plan, but his immediate dislike of the captain was apparent.

The whole night we were busy getting the things on board. Many of Mr. Trelawney's friends came down to bid us a bon voyage and a safe return.

Once all was settled and the crew was safely on board, the Hispaniola pulled the anchor, drew the sails and set sail for the ISLAND OF TREASURE!

Although I was very tired, I did not want to leave the deck. Everything was so new and intriguing. As I was walking along the deck, one of the crewmen called out to Long John Silver, whom they addressed as 'Barbecue', since he was the cook, to sing a song.

"The old one!" cried another.

Long John at once broke into the song I knew so well,

"Fifteen men on the dead man's chest,"

And then the whole crew joined him in the chorus,

"Yo-ho-ho and a bottle of rum!"

The excitement of that moment carried me back to the old Admiral Benbow, and I could almost hear the voice of Captain singing, followed by the chorus.

Chapter 8

The Voyage

I am not going to narrate the voyage in its entirety. It was fairly prosperous. The ship proved to be a good one and the crewmembers were able seamen. The captain thoroughly understood his business. But, towards the end a few things happened, which signaled us that difficult times were ahead.

Mr. Arrow turned out even worse than the captain had apprehended. He had no command over the men and they did what they pleased with him. After a day or two at sea, he began to appear on the deck with hazy eyes, red cheeks, stuttering tongue, and other signs of drunkenness. But we could never make out where he got the drink from, as there were no drinks supplied on the ship. No matter how meticulously we watched him, we could do nothing to solve the mystery.

He was not only incompetent as an officer, but a bad influence amongst the men. And it was plain that, at this rate, he would soon kill himself. So, nobody was much surprised or sorry, when one stormy night Mr. Arrow disappeared and was never seen again; perhaps he fell overboard.

In his absence, the boatswain, Job Anderson, served as the captain's mate.

Mr. Trelawney's knowledge of the sea made him very serviceable. He often took a watch himself in easy weather. And the coxswain, Israel Hands, an experienced old seaman, proved quite useful too.

Long John Silver was the most popular of all the men. The crew respected and obeyed him. He had the art of talking to everybody individually and rendering some particular service to all. To me, he was continually kind and glad whenever I went to the kitchen to talk to him.

"Come, Hawkins," he would say, "come and talk to John. Nobody is more welcome than you, my son. Sit down and hear some good news. Here's Captain Flint. I call my parrot 'Captain Flint', after the famous pirate. Here's Captain Flint predicting that our voyage will be successful."

And his parrot would rattle off, "Pieces of eight! Pieces of eight! Pieces of eight!" till John threw his handkerchief over the cage.

Every man on Hispaniola was very content and they were greatly indulged. If the squire heard that it was any man's birthday, he would order for something special and there was always a barrel of apples for all.

According to our computation, it was the last day of our voyage. We were supposed to reach the Treasure Island by that night, or at the most, by noon the next day. The breeze was steady, and the sea, quiet. Everyone was in the bravest spirits as we were now so near our destination.

Just after sunset, when all my work was over, I felt like having an apple, so I ran to the deck. I got inside the apple barrel and found that there were no apples left. However, sitting there in the dark barrel, and with the rocking of the ship, I soon fell asleep.

Suddenly, I was awakened when a heavy man sat close by, with a rather heavy thud. The barrel shook as he leaned his shoulders against it. I was just about to jump up, when I heard Silver's voice, which was loud and clear.

And before I had heard a dozen words, I started trembling with fear and anxiety. I understood that the lives of all the honest men aboard depended upon me alone.

Chapter 9

The Shocking Truth

o, not I," said Silver. "Flint was the captain; I was his assistant. During that trip I lost my leg and Pew lost his eyes!"

"Ah!" cried a young voice, evidently full of admiration. "Flint was the best of all!"

"I sailed first with England and then with Flint," continued Silver. "I saved nine thousand while I was with England and two thousand while I was with Flint."

So, Silver was a pirate and had been one of Flint's gang!

In the meantime, Silver went on, little doubting that he was being overheard.

"So, where are Flint's men now?" asked the other voice.

"Old Pew is dead," replied Silver, "but the ones alive are on this very ship."

Unbelievable! Our crew comprised of Flint's men! Pirates!

Meanwhile, the cook continued the terrible revelations.

"You see, I am almost fifty," he said, "and once I am back from this cruise, I will settle down as a gentleman."

"Well, I tell you now," replied the young voice, "I didn't like the job at all till I had this talk with you, John, but I am with you now."

At this point Silver gave a whistle and a third man came and sat down with them.

"Dick is with us," Silver told the newcomer.

"I always knew Dick was smart. But there is something I would like to know," said the new voice, which I recognized as Israel Hands'; "how long will we have to wait? When will we attack them?"

"When!" cried Silver. "The last moment I can manage, and that's when! We'll let Captain Smollett, who's a first-grade seaman, sail the ship for us. The squire and doctor have a map, but I don't know where it is, do I? So, what I've planned is this—I want the doctor and the squire to find the treasure for us, and then let the captain sail us back halfway. Then, we will strike."

"But," asked Dick, "after we have beaten them, what are we going to do with them?"

"Well, duty is duty, mates," replied Silver. "As Billy Bones used to say, dead

men don't bite! I give my vote, we will give them death. What I suggest is wait now, but when the time comes, get rid of them!"

By now, I was trembling with fear. I would have leaped out and tried to run away if only I had the strength. Soon, I heard Silver's voice again. He gave a key to Dick and asked him to get some rum to drink. At that instant I realized where Mr. Arrow got all the rum that destroyed him.

Just then, a sort of brightness fell upon me in the barrel, and, looking up, I found that the moon had risen and was shining upon me.

Chapter 10

The Treasure Island

uddenly, there was a great rush across the deck. I could hear people tumbling out from the cabin and the forecastle. I slipped out of the barrel and ran towards the foresail, where all the crew had gathered. Everyone was very excited to see the island, which was becoming clearer as we approached. The fog had disappeared and the moon was visible. Away to the southwest of us we saw two low hills. There was a third peak a few miles away.

So, this was Treasure Island, or, as the pirates called it, The Dead Man's Chest.

I heard Captain Smollett issuing orders to turn the ship just to the east of the island. "And now, men," said the captain, "has any one of you ever seen that land ahead?"

"I have, sir," said Silver. "The ship has to be anchored in the south, behind the island. They call it Skeleton Island. It was once the main place for pirates."

"I have a map here," said Captain Smollett, handing him the map. "See if that's the place."

Silver's eyes gazed sharply as he took the map in his hands, but by the fresh look of the paper he soon realized that this was not the map we had found in Billy Bones' chest. It was an accurate copy, complete in all things, but without the red crosses and the written notes. Silver cleverly concealed his disappointment.

"Yes, sir," he said, "this is the spot."

Then he hobbled away to talk to some of the men.

Meanwhile, the captain went to where the squire and the doctor stood talking. I thought this was the right time to inform them about the danger.

I made my way towards them, and said, "Doctor, get the captain and the squire down to the cabin and then call me there on some pretext. I have terrible news."

The three of them had a little talk and then hurried to the cabin. After some time, they sent for me. I found them seated round a table.

"Now, Hawkins," said the squire, "what is it that you want to tell us?"

I told them all that I had heard in the apple barrel, as briefly as possible.

All three of them listened attentively. At last, when I had finished, the doctor made me sit down beside them, poured me a glass of wine, filled my hands with raisins, and all three drank to my good health, and to my luck and courage.

"Now, captain," said the squire, "you were right, and I was wrong. I now await your orders."

"I am too dumbfounded," said the captain. "I never saw a crew that planned a mutiny, yet not show any signs of it!"

"That's Silver," said the doctor. "He's a remarkable man."

Then the squire and the doctor requested the captain for his advice. The captain acknowledged that they, indeed, were in a bad position, but nevertheless, he had a few suggestions to make.

"First," said he, "we must go on, because if I disclosed anything, they would rebel at once. I suggest that we attack at a moment when they least expect it."

"Can we trust your servants?" the captain asked the squire.

"Yes," replied the squire. "I trust Redruth, Hunter and Joyce as much as myself."

"So that makes it seven of us, including young Hawkins, against nineteen rough seamen," said the captain, thoughtfully.

The appearance of the island, the next morning, was altogether changed. Grey-colored woods covered a large part of the island and streaks of yellow sand could be seen between the trees. The hills ran up clear above the vegetation, and the Spyglass, which was the tallest on the island, ran up sheer from almost every side.

Perhaps it was this melancholy, grey look of the island that made my heart sink. From the first look, I hated the very thought of the Treasure Island, in spite of the shore birds fishing and crying all around us.

We had a dull morning's work before us. The sun shone brightly and there was no wind. The boats had to be taken out and safeguarded and the ship anchored. I volunteered for one of the boats. The heat was sweltering and the men grumbled fiercely over their work. I thought this to be a very bad sign, for up to that day the men had gone dexterously and willingly about their business. But the very sight of the island had relaxed their cords of discipline. They lay about the deck, growling together in talk. The slightest order was received with an unfriendly look and grudgingly and carelessly obeyed. It was evident that mutiny hung over us like a thundercloud. All they seemed to want now was to go ashore on that island of treasure!

The doctor, the squire and the captain were worried about the situation. Around noon, we held a council in the cabin.

"Let's send the men ashore this afternoon," said the captain. "If they all go, we'll take control of the ship. If none of them go, we'll remain in the cabin and pray to God for our safety. If some go, you may be sure that Silver will bring them back again after subduing them. He is as anxious as we are to calm things down!"

Hunter, Joyce and Redruth were taken into our confidence and handed loaded pistols. They received the news with less surprise and a great deal more enthusiasm than we had expected. Then the captain went on deck and addressed the crew.

"My boys," he said, "we've had a hot day and I believe all of you are very tired. Those who want can take the boats and may go ashore for the afternoon."

The gloomy faces of the men at once disappeared and they gave a loud cheer. Silver divided the men in groups and asked six of them to stay on the ship and the rest of the thirteen to go with him to the island. It was clear that Silver was the one in charge.

I also decided to go ashore with the men, as I was not required on the ship at that time. So, I slipped into one of the boats. I thought none of them had noticed me, but as luck would have it, Silver saw me and called out to me.

"Jim, Jim!" I heard him calling out.

I knew I had made a mistake by coming and started regretting my decision.

The crew raced for the beach, but the boat I was in shot far ahead of the others. As it reached the shore-side trees, I caught a branch, swung myself out, and plunged into the nearest wood. I heard Silver call out my name, but I ran straight on till I was out of sight of the boats.

Chapter 11

The Marooned Man

appy that I had finally evaded Silver, I began to enjoy myself in the strange land. The island was uninhabited, and there was nobody for miles around me. The area was sandy and full of trees, with the faraway peaks of hills shining in the sun.

For the first time I felt the joy of exploration. I ran among the tall trees and the small flowering plants. After walking for a while I approached a marsh. Here and

there I saw snakes slithering by; one raised his head from a ledge of rock and hissed at me.

Then I came to a forest full of oak-like trees. The thicket stretched down from the top of one of the sandy hillocks, spreading and growing taller as it went. As I was walking along this place, I heard a loud noise nearby. A wild duck flew up with a quack, another followed and soon, lots of birds started screaming and circling in the air over the whole surface of the marsh.

Almost immediately, I heard faint human voices. I realized that some of the crew members of the ship must be nearby. Crawling on all fours, I proceeded towards the direction of the voices. Then, I recognized Silver's voice! I hid behind some bushes and heard Long John Silver talking to a crewmember, "Friend, you can save your life if you want to. Either join me and have a share in the gold, or die. It is your choice."

"Silver," said the other man, in a shaky voice, "you're old and you're honest, and you've money too. Why do you want to go against these good people? I will never turn against my duty."

Suddenly, the conversation was interrupted by a noise. Faraway out in the marsh, a horrible scream was heard.

Silver's companion was shaken at the sound, but Silver was unperturbed. He stood where he was, resting lightly on his crutch, watching the other man like a snake about to strike.

"John!" cried the other. "What was that?"

"That?" returned Silver, smiling away. "Oh, I think that was Alan."

And at this point, Silver's meek looking companion, Tom, flashed out like a hero.

"Alan!" he cried. "John Silver, you had been a friend of mine, but you are no more now. You've killed Alan, haven't you? Kill

me too, if you can. But I will not join you."
And with that, this brave fellow turned his
back directly on the cook and set off walking
towards the beach. But he was not destined
to go far. John seized the branch of a tree
and threw it at him. It struck the poor man
right between the shoulders, in the middle
of his back. His hands flew up, he gave a

sort of gasp, and fell. John hobbled up to him with an amazing quickness and stabbed him.

For a little while the whole world was spinning before me in a whirling mist and I fainted for the first time in my life.

When I regained consciousness, I saw Silver put his hand into his pocket, bring out a whistle, and blow it. It rang far across the heated air. I realized that with the whistle more men would be coming and I might be discovered. So, I immediately crawled out of the woods and ran back, blindly.

I was completely lost and terrified. I bid goodbye to the Hispaniola, and to the squire, the doctor, and the captain! There was nothing in store for me but death by starvation or at the hands of the mutineers.

I was running very fast, without taking any notice of where I was heading to. As I reached near the foot of a little hill, I saw something that brought me to a total standstill. A gush of gravel came falling down through the trees from the side of the hill and a figure leapt out from behind a tree. But I could not tell whether it was a bear, or man, or a monkey.

Too terrified to even move, I began to recall what I had heard about cannibals. But then I remembered that I had my pistol, and so, mustering up some courage, I walked towards this creature.

As soon as I began to move in its direction, it came out from behind the tree and stepped forward to meet me. The creature was a human being! Then, to my wonder and confusion, he threw himself on his knees in front of me.

"Who are you?" I asked.

"Ben Gunn," he answered, in a hoarse voice. "I am poor Ben Gunn and I have not spoken to anyone in the last three years."

I could now see that he was a white man like me. His skin was burnt by the sun and his lips were black. His fair eyes looked quite startling on his dark face. He was wearing patches of an old ship's canvas, and around his waist he wore an old brass-buckled, leather belt.

"Three years!" I cried. "Were you shipwrecked?"

"No, friend," he said, "I was marooned."

I knew the word stood for a horrible kind of punishment, common among the pirates. The victim would be left on an island, without food and clothes. Most of them never survived.

"Marooned three years ago," he continued, "and lived on goats, berries and oysters since then. But, friend, I am dying to have a good meal. Do you have any cheese with you?"

"If ever I can get aboard again," I said, "I promise, you will have cheese."

All this time, Ben Gunn had been feeling my jacket, smoothing my hands, looking at my boots and generally, in between talking, showing a childish pleasure in the presence of a fellow human being.

"What's your name, friend?" he asked.

"Jim," I told him.

"Jim, Jim," said he, quite pleased. "Now, Jim, I have lived like a poor man on this lonely island. But, let me tell you," his voice almost dropped to a whisper, "I am rich."

I now felt sure that the poor fellow had gone crazy in his isolation. I suppose it must have shown on my face, for he repeated the statement hotly, "Rich! Rich! I'll make you a rich man."

As he said this, a shadow crossed his face. He came closer to me and said, "Jim, you are not Flint's man, are you?"

I immediately realized that he, at least, was not Flint's man, and so I replied, "It's not Flint's ship, and moreover, Flint is dead. But some of Flint's people are there."

"Is there a man with one leg?" he gasped.

"Yes, he is there. He's the cook and the leader of the rest too."

As he heard this, he almost twisted my hand in anger. But when I told him the whole story of our voyage, he was happy to be my friend.

"Would your captain give me a safe passage home?" he asked, shrewdly.

"Why not?" I cried. "The squire's a gentleman and I am sure he would gladly help you. And besides, we would need help on the ship on the way back."

On hearing this, Ben Gunn seemed very much relieved.

"I was on Flint's ship when he buried the treasure on the island," said Ben Gunn. "He was with six other strong seamen. He had gone to bury the treasure. We were on the ship waiting for him. Long John and Billy

Bones were also on the ship with me. One day, Flint came back all alone. He had killed the six men and buried them. So, no one knew where Flint buried his treasure. When we asked where the treasure was, all he said was, 'Ah, you can go ashore, if you like and stay and hunt for it'."

"I came back after three years, but in another ship. I told the men on the ship that this was the place where Flint's treasure was buried. We anchored the ship and came ashore. We hunted for the treasure for twelve days, but in vain. Then one day, the others came to me angrily, handed me a gun, a spade, and a pickaxe. 'You may stay here and hunt for Flint's treasure'," they told me and left.

"Well, there's a boat that I made myself. I keep it under the white rock. We might try that after dark."

Suddenly, we heard the thunder of cannon.

"What's that?" Ben Gunn cried out.

"They have begun to fight!" I cried. "Follow me!"

I began to run towards the anchorage, with Ben Gunn close at my side. After sometime, I saw in front of me the Union Jack fluttering in the air above the wood.

Chapter 12

The Doctor's Narrative

t was around half past one, when the captain, the squire and I were talking in the cabin. At that moment, Hunter came with the news that Jim Hawkins had slipped into a boat and had gone to the island.

Although we never doubted Jim's honesty, we were bothered about his security. We ran on the deck. The six remaining villains were sitting grumbling under a sail in the forecastle. On the shores, we could see the boats tied up and a man sitting in each. One of them was whistling 'Lillibullero'.

After consulting the squire and the captain, I decided to go ashore with Hunter to seek information.

As we headed ashore in the jolly boat, in the direction of the stockade marked upon the chart, we saw two of the men who were guarding the boats, glance at us. But they didn't move from their place, as maybe, they were ordered not to leave their position.

Once we reached the island, I jumped out of the boat with a pistol in hand and began walking towards the thicket lying ahead. I had not gone a hundred yards when I reached the stockade. The building at once caught my fancy. It was a large blockhouse of logs, equipped with firing ports, enclosing a clear spring of water, and itself enclosed by a strong six-foot fence without an opening. As this structure was near the top of a hill, a small group could very well hold off a much larger force, indefinitely, if they had enough food and ammunition.

As all these thoughts were passing through my mind, suddenly, I heard a shrill cry of a man at the point of death.

I was not new to death, but for a moment my heart stopped beating.

'Jim Hawkins is gone,' was my first thought.

Hunter and I immediately came back to the ship. The squire, too, had heard the gunshot, and had turned as white as a sheet, thinking of the harm he had led us to!

We decided to immediately attack the pirates on board. We put old Redruth in the gallery, with three or four loaded guns to guard the six pirates on board, while Joyce and I loaded the jolly boat with powder tins, guns, bags of biscuits and my bag of medicines.

In the meantime, the squire and the captain stayed on the deck and the latter welcomed Israel Hands, who was the principal man aboard.

"Mr. Hands," he said, "here are two of us with a pistol each. If any one of you make a signal, that man's dead."

They were a good deal taken aback, but when they saw the captain and the squire on deck, and Redruth waiting for them too, they remained silent.

Once we had the jolly boat loaded, Hunter, Joyce, and I journeyed towards the stockade again, as fast as oars could take us. After the whole cargo was ashore safely, Hunter and Joyce took up their position in the stockade and I came back to the Hispaniola.

The squire was waiting for me at the rear window. We picked one gun and a knife for each one of us and threw the rest of the ammunitions overboard, so that the pirates would not be able to use them.

"Now, men," said the captain, addressing the six men, "do you hear me?"

There was no answer from the forecastle.

"It's to you, Abraham Gray. I am speaking to you," resumed Mr. Smollett, a little louder. "I am leaving this ship, and I order you to follow your captain. I know you are a good man at heart. I give you thirty seconds to join me in."

Again, there was no answer!

"Come, my fine fellow," continued the captain. "Don't wait so long. I am risking my life as well as the lives of these good gentlemen every second."

There was a sudden scuffle and Abraham Gray burst out with a knife cut on one side of his cheek.

"I am with you, sir," he said to the captain.

The next moment, he and the captain had dropped into the boat and headed towards the shore.

The little jolly boat that we were in was gravely overloaded. Five grown men, plus the powder, pork and bread-bags was more than the boat was meant to carry. Several times we moved a little in the water. Such was the situation that we were even afraid to breathe.

Suddenly, the captain spoke up. "The cannon!" he said.

We had entirely forgotten the cannon. Not only that, but I recalled at the same moment that the round-shot and the powder for the cannon, too, had been left behind.

"Israel was Flint's gunner," said Gray, hoarsely.

I could hear as well as see Israel Hands plumping down a round-shot on the deck.

"Who's the best shot?" asked the captain.

"Mr. Trelawney," I said.

"Mr. Trelawney, will you please bring down one of these men for me? Hands, if possible," said the captain.

The squire was as cool as steel. He raised his gun and we leaned over to the other side to keep the balance, all was so nicely planned that we did not lose equilibrium when the shot was fired. But, unluckily, just as Trelawney fired, Hands stooped down, the ball whistled over him and it was one of the other four who fell! The cry he gave was echoed by a great number of voices from the shore. Looking in that direction I saw the other pirates trooping out from among the trees and tumbling into the boats.

"We must hurry!" cried the captain. "If we can't get ashore, all will be over."

"Only one of the boats is being manned, sir," I added. "The crew of the other is most likely going round the shore to avoid us."

Thirty or forty strokes and we would reach the shore. That very moment another shot fired, by Israel Hands, passed over our heads. We backed off, trying to save ourselves from the shot. As a result of our backing off, the boat sank by the stern in three feet of water. All our stores sank to the bottom of the sea and three out of our five guns were ruined!

To add to our concern, we heard voices drawing near us in the woods along the shore. We wadded ashore as fast as we could, leaving behind us the poor jolly boat and half of all our powder and provisions.

We hastened across the strip of wood that now divided us from the stockade and at every step we took, the voices of the pirates sounded nearer. Observing Gray to be unarmed, I handed him my sword. It was heartening to see him knit his brows and make the blade swing through the air. It was plain from every line of his body that our new companion was worth his salt.

Another forty steps, and we would come to the edge of the wood. We saw the stockade in front of us. We were about to enter the enclosure from the middle of the south side, when seven mutineers burst out at the southwestern corner.

On coming face to face with us, the pirates paused for a while in surprise. Before they recovered, not only the squire and I, but Hunter and Joyce from the stockade had time to fire. One of our enemies fell, and the rest turned and disappeared into the woods.

As we began to rejoice over our good success (the fallen pirate was dead), a ball whistled close past my ear and poor Tom Redruth stumbled and fell on the ground. Both the squire and I fired back, but we had nothing to aim at. Then, we turned our attention to poor Tom.

The captain and Gray were already examining him and I saw with half an eye that nothing could be done. Without any further examination, we carried the old gamekeeper into the log-house.

The squire dropped down beside him on his knees and kissed his hand, crying like a child. Not long after, Tom passed away.

In the meantime, the captain had found a cut-down fir tree lying in the enclosure, and with the help of Hunter, he had set it up at the corner of the log-house where the trunks crossed and made an angle. Then, climbing on the roof, he hoisted the British flag. This seemed to relieve him a lot. He re-entered the log-house and came forward with another flag and reverently spread it on the body.

"Don't be upset, sir," he said, shaking the squire's hand. "All's well with him. He died doing his duty."

Then, the captain pulled me aside. "Our stores should be uncovered," he said. "Someone should go and bring in the meat."

Gray and Hunter stole out of the stockade, but it proved a useless mission. Four or five of the mutineers were already there, busy carrying off our stores. Silver was their commander and every man had mysteriously attained a musket from somewhere. Meanwhile, I kept wondering over poor Jim Hawkins' fate. Suddenly, there was a call on the other side.

"Somebody is hailing us," said Hunter, who was on guard.

"Doctor! Squire! Captain! Hullo, Hunter, is that you?" cried a familiar voice.

I ran to the door in time to see Jim Hawkins, safe and sound, climbing over the stockade.

Chapter 13

Jim's Story

s soon as Ben Gunn saw the flag, he came to a halt. He stopped me by the arm and sat down.

"Here are your friends, sure enough," he said.

"I doubt if it is them. I believe it is the pirates," I replied.

"If it was Silver, he would surely fly the pirate flag, the Jolly Roger. No, these are your friends. There was firing too. Let us hope your friends are in the stockade that was built years ago by Flint."

"I should hurry and join my friends then," I said.

"When you want to see Ben Gunn, just come to the place where you met him today," said Ben. "Whosoever comes, should come with a white flag in hand. And don't forget to send that person alone. Ben Gunn has reasons of his own."

"Well," said I, "I believe I understand. You have something to offer and you wish to see the squire or the doctor and you will be found where I found you today. Is that all?"

"Yes."

"Good," I said, "and now, may I go?"

"You won't forget?" he inquired, anxiously.

At that moment, we heard the firing of a cannon, and a cannonball landed a few yards away from us. Immediately, both of us fled the spot. Ben Gunn ran in one direction and I in the other. There was a great deal of fighting going on. I moved from one hiding place to another. After creeping down among the shore-side trees, finally the Hispaniola came into sight. It was still there where we had anchored it, but with the Jolly Roger

flying high in the air. Near the shore I saw some of Silver's men destroying something with an axe. Later on, I came to know that it was the poor jolly boat.

As I walked on the shore, I could still hear the volley of cannons going on. Then, at some distance, I saw an isolated rock, pretty high and peculiarly white in color, rising from among the low bushes. It occurred to me that this might be the white rock, which Ben Gunn had spoken of. I now knew that if some day I needed a boat, where to look for it. Walking along the side of the wood, I finally reached the shoreward side of the stockade.

My friends were shocked as well as pleasantly surprised to see me alive. I was warmly welcomed back into the party. I soon told them my story and began to look around the cabin. The log-house was made of trunks of pine. There was a porch at the door, and under this porch there was a little spring. I noticed that little had been left besides the framework of the house. In one corner there was a stone slab laid down as a hearth, and an old rusty iron basket to check the fire. The captain then called us all, gave us work to do, and divided us into units. The doctor, Gray and I were in one group, and the squire, Hunter and Joyce were in the other. Two of us were sent to fetch firewood and the doctor was made the cook. The captain kept on talking cheerfully to keep our spirits alive.

The cold evening breeze whistled through every crack of the old building and sprinkled the floor with a continual rain of fine sand. There was sand in our eyes, sand in our teeth and sand in our food. Our chimney was a square hole in the roof, and it was of little help in keeping the smoke out. And so, all the smoke kept us coughing.

From time to time the doctor came to the door for a little air and to rest his eyes and whenever he did so, he exchanged a few words with me.

"Is this Ben Gunn a sane man?" he asked once.

"I do not know, sir," I said. "I am not very sure whether he's sane."

The doctor said that a man who had been marooned for three years, cannot be altogether sensible. He then told me that he had saved some cheese for Ben Gunn. After supper, as we sat discussing our plans, we could hear the pirates roaring and singing late into the night. I was dead tired and when I retired to sleep, I slept like a log of wood. The next morning, I was awakened by a hustle and bustle.

"Ceasefire!" I heard someone say and then, with a cry of surprise, "Silver himself!"

I jumped up and, rubbing my eyes, ran to a peephole in the wall.

Chapter 14

The Fireworks

here were two men just outside the stockade. One of them was waving a white cloth and the other man was Long John Silver himself.

The captain gave us instructions to be alert.

"Dr. Livesey, take the north side, if you please; Jim, the east; Gray, west. Be careful!"

And then, he turned to the mutineers.

"What do you want?"

"Captain Silver wishes to make terms," said the other pirate.

"Captain Silver! Who's he?" cried the captain.

"Me, sir! These poor boys have chosen me as their captain after you deserted us, sir," Long John answered, laying a particular emphasis upon the word 'deserted'. "We're willing to submit, if we can come to terms."

The captain made it clear that if Silver wished to talk, he could come to our cabin, but if there was any treachery on the pirates' part, then Silver would have to pay with his life.

The steep incline, the thick tree stumps and the soft sand made the climb very difficult for Silver and his crutch. But he stuck to it like a man in silence, and at last arrived before the captain and saluted him. Then, both the men sat down to talk.

Silver put in his terms, "What I wanted to tell you is that we want the treasure. If you want to save your lives, you give us the map. And in return, we will spare your lives and let you come aboard along with us. But if you wish to stay here, you may and the first ship we meet, we will send them here to take you home."

Captain Smollett rose from his seat and knocked out the ashes of his pipe in the palm of his left hand.

"Is that all you had to say?" said the captain. "Now you'll hear ME. If you'll come up one by one, unarmed, I'll take you home to England. But if you don't, be sure that I'll have you all hung! You don't have the map and so can't find the treasure. You can't fight us, for our man, Gray, got away from the five of yours! You won't be able to sail the ship back safely. Now, Master Silver, these are the last good words you'll get from me. The next time I see you, I will kill you."

Silver's face became red with anger and he cried, "Give me a hand!"

"Not I," returned the captain.

"Who'll give me a hand?" he roared.

None of us moved, and finally, crawling on the sand, Silver managed to get hold of his crutch and stood up. Then he spat into the spring.

"There!" he cried. "That's what I think of you. In an hour, I will attack you and the lucky ones will die." Angrily, he stumbled off and disappeared among the trees.

Once Silver left, the captain came in and said, "My boys, Silver is going to attack in an hour. We're outnumbered, but if we fight in shelter, I've no doubt that we can beat them."

First, the captain told me to have my breakfast and asked Hunter to give all the others a round of brandy. Then, all of us got ready for the attack. The doctor was positioned at the door and asked not to expose himself. He was also instructed to fire through the porch.

Hunter took up the east side and Joyce stood by the west side.

"Mr. Trelawney, you are the best in aiming shots. You and Gray will cover this

long north side with the five loopholes, it's there that the danger is. Hawkins, neither you nor I are good at shooting. We'll stand by to load the guns and bear a hand."

We stood in our positions, in a fever of heat and anxiety. An hour passed away, till suddenly, Joyce whipped up his musket and fired. This was immediately followed by a volley of gunshots. The shots rained from every side of the enclosure. Several bullets struck the log-house, but not one entered. As the smoke cleared away and vanished, the stockade and the woods around it looked as quiet and empty as before.

Suddenly, few pirates leaped from the woods on the north side and ran straight to the stockade. At the same moment, the gunfire was once more opened from the woods and a rifle bullet hit the doctor's gun, shattering it to pieces. Silver's men jumped over the fence like monkeys. Squire and Gray fired again and three of our enemies fell.

Four men had succeeded in entering our territory, while the ones in the thicket continued firing at us. In a moment, the four pirates had crossed the hillock and were upon us. One of them grasped Hunter's gun from his hand and hit him unconscious through the window. Meanwhile, another appeared suddenly in the doorway and fell with his sword on the doctor.

The log-house, to which we owed our comparative safety, was, by now, full of smoke, cries, confusion and pistol-shots. And then, suddenly, we heard the captain shouting, "Out lads, out and fight them in the open!"

I snatched a sword from the pile and at that moment someone gave me a cut across the knuckles. I dashed out of the door into the clear sunlight. Someone was close behind me. With my sword raised, I ran round the corner of the house. The very next moment I was face to face with Anderson. He roared aloud and the sword in his hand went up above his head, flashing in the sunlight. I leaped in a flash upon one side and then, suddenly, I lost my footing in the soft sand and rolled headlong down the slope.

When I found my feet again, the fight was over and the victory was ours.

The doctor, Gray and I ran inside the stockade for shelter. The house was, by now, a bit cleared of smoke and we saw at a glance the price we had paid for victory. Three pirates were dead, Hunter was lying unconscious and Joyce was dead.

Right in the center, the squire was supporting the wounded captain, each one as pale as the other.

Chapter 15

My Sea Adventure

Hunter never regained his consciousness and quietly passed away the next night. As for the captain, his wounds were grievous indeed, but not dangerous. He was sure to recover, the doctor said, but in the meantime and for weeks to come, he was advised not to walk or to move his arm. My own accidental cut across the knuckles was nothing. Doctor Livesey patched it up with plaster. After having some food, the squire and the doctor sat with the captain, discussing what to do next. After some time, the doctor took up his hat and pistols, put the chart in his pocket and with a gun over his shoulder, set off briskly through the trees.

Gray and I were sitting together at the far end of the stockade.

"Where is the doctor going to?" he asked.

"If I am right, he's going to see Ben Gunn," I said.

I was right, as it appeared later. In the meantime, I began to get another thought into my head, which was not by any means so right. What I began to do was to envy the doctor walking in the cool shadow of the woods, with the birds about him and the pleasant smell of the pines, while I sat with my clothes sticking to my perspiring back. Blood smeared about me and many poor dead bodies lay all around. I took a strong dislike to the whole place.

I noticed that no one was observing me. I took this opportunity to escape from the stockade. I filled my pockets with biscuits, picked up a pistol and sneaked out quietly for the white rock I had seen last evening.

I took to the east coast of the island. Although still warm and sunny, it was quite late in the afternoon. As I continued to walk through the woods, I could hear from far the continuous thunder of the foamy sea. Soon, cool draughts of air began to reach me and after a few steps further I came forth into the open borders of the grove. And there, I saw the sea lying ahead of me, with the waves lashing and tossing its foam along the beach.

I walked along the shore with great enjoyment, till I was almost to the south of the island. I saw the Hispaniola floating still and along with it lay one of the rowboats. I was shocked to recognize Silver's figure in the boat. Soon after, I saw the boat heading for the shore. There were two men leaning over the ship, one with a red cap on. As soon as Silver's boat left, they went down into the cabin. Just about the same time, the sun had gone down and as the fog was collecting rapidly, it began to grow dark. I knew I had no time to lose if I were to find Ben Gunn's boat.

I had, in the meantime, formed a plan in my mind, to slip out under the cover of the

night, cut the Hispaniola loose and let her go adrift.

I waited for darkness and made a hearty meal of biscuits. Once it was completely dark, I began my search for the white rock.

I finally found Ben Gunn's boat, a crude, lopsided framework of tough wood. But the great advantage of the boat was that it was very light. It was a very safe boat for a person of my height and weight.

But when I had pushed the boat into the water, I saw that it was difficult to handle. Ben Gunn himself had admitted that his little boat was 'queer to handle, till you knew her way', which I certainly did not know. The boat turned in every direction, but not in the one I had to go. Luckily, the tide swept me down towards the Hispaniola.

When I was only a few yards from the Hispaniola, I could see the yellow lantern light shining out. As I moved a little closer, I heard the sound of loud voices from the cabin. One I recognized as that of Israel Hands. The other was, of course, of the red cap. Both men seemed drunk as well as furiously angry. Oaths flew like hailstones and every now and then there occurred such an explosion that they finally ended in blows. Then, there was silence.

At this very moment a breeze swept through, and I was almost instantly hit against the bows of the Hispaniola. I now tried to cut the ropes that anchored the ship, with my gully knife and after a lot of effort, finally managed to sever the cord. Then suddenly, my hands came across a light cord that was trailing overboard. Instantly, I grasped it. Why I should have done so, I can hardly explain. It was at first mere instinct, but once I had it in my hands, curiosity began to take the better of me and I was determined to see what was happening on the ship!

Chapter 16

To the Island Again

somehow, managed to climb the ship and land on the deck. I looked around but saw no one at first. And then, I saw the red cap lying on the cabin floor. He was obviously dead. Israel Hands was propped against the bulwarks, with his chin on his chest and his face white. There was blood on the floor and I thought they had both killed each other in their fight.

While I was looking and wondering, Israel Hands turned, with a low moan.

So, he was alive!

Hearing his moans of agony, I felt pity for the man. But when I remembered the talk I had overheard from the apple barrel, all pity left me. I walked up to him.

"Hello, Mr. Hands," I said, ironically.

Israel Hand's eyes rolled round, but he was too weak to express surprise. All he could do was to mutter, "Brandy."

I went down to the cellar and found a bottle of brandy for Hands and for myself, I dug out some biscuits, pickled fruits, a great bunch of raisins and a piece of cheese. With these, I went back on deck, put down my own supply, well out of the coxswain's reach, had a good deep drink of water and then gave Hands the brandy. He must have drunk almost a quarter of the bottle before he took it away from his mouth. "I've come aboard to take possession of this ship, Mr. Hands," I told him. "And you'll please regard me as your captain, until further notice."

Hands gave me a sour look, but said nothing. After this, the first thing I did was to bring down the pirate flag. Hands watched me keenly and slyly, his chin on the chest all the while. At last, he spoke up, "I think, Captain Hawkins, you'll now want to get to the shore. So, I think we should make a deal."

Accordingly, Hands and I made a pact. I agreed to give him food and drinks and my scarf to tie his wound with and in turn, he agreed to help me in sailing the ship back. In a few minutes, I had the Hispaniola sailing easily along the coast of Treasure Island. In between sailing, I took out a soft silk handkerchief and bound the wound in Hand's thigh. I also gave him food and drinks as promised and before long, he looked a lot better. He sat up straighter and spoke louder and clearer.

The breeze helped the ship. As we sailed, I noticed a treacherous smile on Israel Hands' face. We were sitting in silence over a meal, waiting for the tide to move in when Hands told me that he would like to have wine instead of brandy.

Now, preferring wine over brandy was something so very unnatural for a pirate that I became suspicious of Hands' intentions at once. I realized that he just wanted me to get away from the deck.

"All right," I answered. "I'll bring you wine, Mr. Hands. But I'll have to go down and search for it."

With that I walked away with all the noise I could. As soon as I was out of his sight, I quietly hid myself and watched him from my hiding place.

The worst of my suspicions came true.

Hands had grown much stronger than he had revealed to me. He got up from his place with little difficulty, pulled out a long knife from beneath a coil of rope and concealed it in his pocket. And then he came back and lay down where he was before.

So, Israel Hands could walk about now! And he was armed too! But at the same time I was also sure that he would not harm me until we had anchored the ship.

With all these troubling thoughts in my mind, I went to the cabin and returned with a bottle of wine. Hands lay as I had left him, with his eyelids lowered as though he were too weak to bear the light. He, however, managed to look up at me and thanked me for the wine.

We were, by now, just two miles away from the shore. Hands gave me the instructions and I steered accordingly. And soon, we were ashore.

In my excitement of reaching the land, I had quite forgotten about the danger that hung above my head and stood leaning over the ship's bulwarks, watching the ripples of the waves. Perhaps, I had heard a creak,

or seen his shadow moving from the tail of my eye, or perhaps it was my instinct, but, sure enough, when I looked round, there was Hands, with his knife in his hand coming straight at me!

We both must have cried out aloud when our eyes met. At the same instant, Hands threw himself forward and I leapt sideways towards the bows. As I did so, I let go of the rudder, which struck Hands across the chest and stopped him. Before he could recover, I was out of the corner where he had trapped me. I remembered the pistols in the pocket of my jacket, and taking one out I aimed at Hands. The hammer fell, but there followed neither flash nor sound. I cursed myself for my neglect. Why hadn't I, long before now, reloaded my only weapons?

At that very moment, the Hispaniola hit land and tilted a bit on one side. As a result, both Hands and I fell over. However, I was the first to get up. The sudden tilting of the ship had made the deck unsuitable for running. I had to find some new way of escape. Quick as lightning, I climbed the mast and did not draw a breath till I was seated in the crows nest. Now, I tried quickly to reload both my pistols, at the same time keeping an eye on Hands, who was slowly advancing towards me with the knife in his hand. And then, he began to mount the mast. By the time he had climbed more than a third of the way up, I finished loading both my pistols, aimed them at Hands and cried out, "One more step, Mr. Hands, and I'll blow your brains out!"

He stopped instantly. I saw that he was trying to think, but suddenly, his right hand went over the back of his shoulder. In a moment, something flew like an arrow through the air and cut deep into my shoulder. In the horrid pain and surprise of the moment, both my pistols went off and fell from my hands. But they did not fall alone, for with a choked cry, Israel Hands' head plunged into the water.

Chapter 17

The Big Surprise

srael Hands was dead. I began to feel sick, weak and terrified. Hot blood was running over my back and chest. I shuddered violently in pain. I came down from the mast and did what I could to my wounds. Then, I brought down the ship's sails so that it would not be blown about by the wind, climbed over the side of the ship and waded ashore.

I was quite proud of myself for having recaptured the Hispaniola. All I wanted now was to get back to my friends as quickly as possible and tell them of my victory.

So, in high spirits, I headed towards the direction of the log-house. Up till now it was quite dark. But then, a sudden brightness fell upon me and looking up I saw that the moon had risen. I proceeded rapidly, sometimes walking, sometimes running. At last, I reached the borders of the clearing in front of the stockade. I saw that on the other side of the house an immense fire had burned itself into clear embers. There was nobody around. I got upon my hands and knees and crawled, without a sound, towards the corner of the house. As I drew nearer, my heart was suddenly lightened as I heard my friends snoring loudly and peacefully in their sleep.

I softly opened the door and thought of quietly creeping in to where my place was. I chuckled to think of the surprised look that would surface on my friends' faces when they would find me the next morning.

Just then, my foot struck something, it was a sleeping man's leg and he turned and groaned, but did not wake up.

And then, all of a sudden, the silence was broken by a shrill voice, "Pieces of eight! Pieces of eight! Pieces of eight!"

It was Silver's green parrot, Captain Flint!

I had no time left to recover. Silver woke up and cried, "Who's there?"

I turned to run and struck violently against somebody. I fell into the arms of a second person, who held me tight.

"Bring a torch, Dick," said Silver's voice.

In the light of the torch, I saw that the pirates were in possession of the stockade and stores. So, it was not my friends', but my enemies' house into which I had so willingly walked!

In the meantime, I did not see any prisoners and this increased my misery. I was sure that all my friends had been killed by these men.

There were six pirates. Five of them had stood up and the sixth had only risen upon his elbow, he was deadly pale. The bloodstained bandage round his head made it clear that he had been recently wounded and dressed.

"So," cried Silver, "here's Jim Hawkins, shiver my timbers! Dropped in for a visit, eh? Welcome."

I stood with my back against the wall, looking at Silver's face.

"Now you see, Jim, as you are here," said he, "I'll give you a piece of my mind. I've always liked you, for I thought you were a spirited boy and the picture of my own self when I was young and handsome. I always wanted you to join us and take your share and now, my cheeky fellow, you've got to."

"Well, I have the right to know why you're here and where my friends are!" I cried, indignantly.

Silver replied to me in a gracious tone, "Yesterday morning, Mr. Hawkins, Doctor Livesey came down with a flag of truce. He said, 'Captain Silver, the ship's gone.' We went and looked and found that the ship was indeed gone! So, we bargained. The doctor gave us the cabin and all the stores and the firewood. As for them, they left and I don't know where they are."

He puffed away at his pipe for a few seconds and then continued his speech.

"And let me tell you, according to the bargain you were left to us. When I asked

him, 'How many of you are there?' he answered, 'Four and one of us wounded. As for that boy, I don't know where he is, nor do I care. We're sick of him'."

"Is that all?" I asked.

"Yes, that is all," he replied.

"And now I am to choose?"

"And now you are to choose," said Silver.

"Well," I said, "then let me tell you a few things. All of you here are in a very bad state, ship lost, treasure lost, men lost, your whole business gone to wreck and if you want to know who did it, you will be surprised to know that it was I who did it! I was in the apple barrel the night we sighted land and I heard you, John. I heard all that you, Dick and Hands talked about. And I went and told every word you said to the captain and the rest.

That is not all. I took your ship to a place where you will not find her. I cut her cable and killed your men. So, if you now think that I am afraid of you, let me tell you that I AM NOT!"

None of them moved. They were totally astounded and then suddenly, Morgan, one of the pirates, drew his knife and sprang at me.

Silver stopped him. "Who are you, Tom Morgan? Maybe you thought you are the captain here. Stop where you are. Let me remind you that I am your captain here! "

Morgan paused, but the others opposed.

"Tom's right," said one. "We should kill this brat."

"I am not going to be fooled by you every time, John Silver," added another.

"If any of you wants to fight me, I am ready for it!" roared Silver. "Take a sword, whosoever dares and I'll see how brave you are!"

Not a man stirred or answered.

"That's your spirit, is it?" he added, returning his pipe to his mouth. "Well, I am the captain here and I know that none of you are good seamen. I like that boy now. He's more a man than any of you in this house here. If any one of you lay a hand on him, you will have me to face."

Silver leaned back against the wall, his arms crossed and his pipe in the corner of his mouth. He was as calm as though he had been to a church, yet his eyes kept wandering cautiously. There was a long pause after this. The men drew together towards the far end of the log-house, whispering continuously.

"You seem to have a lot to say," remarked Silver. "Speak up and let me hear it."

"We ask your pardon, sir," replied one of the men, "this crew's dissatisfied. And by your own rules, I believe we can step outside for a council and talk together." With that, he, followed by the rest of the men, saluted Silver and stepped outside.

The sea-cook instantly removed his pipe and hopped over to my side.

"Now, look here, Jim Hawkins," he said, in a whisper, "you're a few inches away from death. They're going to throw me off and plan to kill you. But, do not worry, I'll stand by you through thick and thin."

I dimly began to understand.

"I'll do whatever I can. I promise you that," I said.

"It's a bargain!" cried Long John.

He hobbled to the torch, lighted his pipe and then continued, "And Jim, tell me something, why did the doctor give me the map?"

I was taken aback by this and Silver understood that I had no idea about it.

"Ah, well, he did, though," he said. "And there's something behind that, no doubt, something good or bad, Jim."

Chapter 18

Mutiny within Mutiny

he council of pirates lasted for some time. Then the door opened and the five men pushed one of their comrades forward. The man stepped forth, passed something into Silver's hand and slipped smartly back again amongst his companions.

Silver looked at what had been given to him.

"The Black Spot!" he observed. "I had thought so."

"Come, now," said George, "you can't fool this crew any more. You've messed up this cruise. You let the enemy out of this trap here. You did not let us attack them and now you want to keep this boy alive too."

"Is that all?" asked Silver, quietly. "Well now, I'll answer all these points. Look there and you will know why I did it all."

And he pointed down to a paper, lying on the floor, that I instantly recognized. It was none other than the map on yellow paper, with the three red crosses that I had found in the oilcloth at the bottom of Captain's chest! I could not believe my eyes. Why did the doctor give him this?

But as it perplexed me, the appearance of the map was unbelievable to the surviving mutineers. They leaped upon it, like cats upon a mouse. It went from hand to hand; one tearing it from another, accompanied with cries and laughter.

Silver suddenly sprang up. He knew that the tide had once again turned in his favor. "Now I warn you, George!" he cried. "One more word from you, and I'll fight you."

"That's fair enough," said the old man, Morgan.

"Fair! I believe so," said the sea-cook. "You lost the ship, I found the treasure. And now I resign! Elect the one you wish to be your captain now. I am done with it."

"Silver!" they cried out in unison. "Barbecue is our captain!"

That was where the whole discussion ended. Soon after, all of the pirates enjoyed a round of drinks and lay down to sleep. But it took a long time to close an eye. I saw clearly the remarkable game that Silver now indulged in, keeping the mutineers together on one hand and on the other, grasping every means, possible and impossible, to save his miserable life.

The next morning I was awakened by a clear, hearty voice greeting us from the outskirts of the wood, "Here's the doctor."

I was very happy to hear this, but at the same time I was ashamed to go and meet him. I knew he had lost all faith in me.

And then I ran to a window and looked out. I saw Doctor Livesey standing in front of Silver. He had come to examine the wounded pirate.

"A very good morning to you, doctor!" cried Silver, beaming with good nature. He stood on the hilltop with his crutch under his arm, quite the old John in voice, manner and expression.

"We've quite a surprise for you, sir," Silver continued. "We've a little stranger here!"

I could hear the alteration in the doctor's voice as he said, "Not Jim?"

"Yes! The very same Jim," said Silver.

The doctor stopped shocked and it was quite a few seconds before he seemed able to move on.

"Well, well," he said at last, "duty first, pleasure later. Let me have a look at these patients of yours."

A moment later, the doctor had entered the log-house. He looked at me grimly and then turned to attend the patient.

"Dick is unwell, sir," said one.

"Is he?" replied the doctor. "Well, step up here, Dick and let me see your tongue."

"Well," he said, after the pirates had taken his prescriptions, more like charity schoolchildren than pirates, "well, that's done for today. And now I would like to have a talk with that boy, please."

"Doctor," said Silver, "you just wait outside the stockade and I'll bring the boy to you."

Silver and I walked across the sand to where the doctor awaited us and as soon as we were within speaking distance, Silver stopped.

"Let me tell you, doctor," he said, "and the boy will also tell you how I saved his life. And do not forget our bargain."

Saying this, Silver stepped back and waited for me.

"So, Jim," said the doctor, sadly, "here you are. As you have sowed, so shall you reap, my boy!"

At that point, I broke down and tears rolled down my cheeks.

"Doctor," I said, "I have blamed myself enough. I should have been dead by now if Silver hadn't stood for me. I can die and I think I deserve it, but what I fear is torture. If they come to torture me ..."

"Jim," the doctor interrupted and his voice was quite changed, "Jim, I can't have this. I cannot let you stay here. Jump over and we'll run for it."

"No, doctor," I replied, "I know that neither you nor the squire would do anything like this and I too would not do anything such. Silver trusted me. I gave my word and so I will go back. But first, I have to tell you something important. I got the ship and she lies in the North Inlet on the southern beach, just below high water. At half tide she must be high and dry."

"The ship!" exclaimed the doctor. He couldn't believe his ears.

I described to him my adventures in a few words and he heard me out in silence.

"There is a kind of fate in this," he observed, when I had finished. "In every step it's you who have saved our lives and do you suppose, by any chance that we are going to let you lose yours? That would be immoral, my boy. You found out the plot; you found Ben Gunn, the best deed that you ever did, or will ever do. Silver!" he cried. "Silver! I'll give you a piece of advice," he continued, as the cook drew near again. "Don't you be in any great hurry after that treasure. And if we both get out, I'll do my best to save you from the law." Silver's face was radiant. "Thank you, sir," he said. "I believe you. I am sure, sir."

Dr. Livesey shook hands with me through the fence, nodded to Silver and set off into the wood.

Chapter 19

Flint's Compass

im," said Silver, when we were alone, "if I saved your life, you saved mine and I'll not forget it. I saw the doctor asking you to jump over the fence and run away with him and I also saw you stand by your word. And now, Jim, we will go hunting for this treasure. We must stick together and keep a close watch on the others."

Just then a man called us for breakfast. They had lit a fire suitable to roast an ox.

The food was three times more than what we could eat. All the men ate their fill and threw the leftovers into the fire.

I was now pretty sure that Long John Silver would leave the pirates for freedom and wealth. I was very confused at the behavior of my friends and their leaving the cabin and giving up the map to the pirates. If there was a plan in it, it was completely incomprehensible to me.

After breakfast, all of us set out. Captain Flint sat perched upon Silver's shoulder and rattled purposeless sea-talk. I followed Silver. I had a rope about my waist and Silver held the loose end of the rope in his hand. I was led like a dancing bear. The other men carried picks and shovels and a few others were loaded with pork, bread and brandy for the midday meal.

Thus, we all set out, one after another, in the direction of the hill marked Spy Glass, following the directions on the map.

Tall tree, shoulder, bearing a point to the N. of N.N.E

Skeleton Island E.S.E. and by E

Ten feet

Right before us was a plateau of about two to three hundred feet. The top of the plateau was dotted thickly with pine-trees of varying height. However, the question was, amidst all these tall trees, which one was the particular 'tall tree' of Captain Flint? In the beginning, the ground was marshy and was quite difficult for exploring, but slowly as we climbed up, it grew more open. Thickets of green nutmeg-trees grew alongside the broad shadow of the pines. We walked for quite some time and then landed at the mouth of a river that ran down a woody cleft of the Spyglass. Then, turning to our left, we began to ascend the slope towards the plateau. We were approaching the edge of the plateau, when one of the men, who was walking ahead of us, cried aloud in terror.

Hearing his cry, we began racing in his direction.

"He couldn't possibly have found the treasure," said old Morgan, hurrying past us.

Indeed, when we reached the spot, it was something very different. At the foot of a big, tall pine, a human skeleton lay on the ground. A few shreds of clothing were on it.

A chill struck my heart.

"He was a seaman," said George Merry, who, bolder than the rest, had gone up close and was examining the rags of clothing.

"Yes, yes," said Silver, "but why is the skeleton lying in this manner? It is not

natural. Indeed, on a second glance, it seemed impossible to fancy that the body was in a natural position. The man lay perfectly straight—his feet pointing in one direction and his hands, raised above his head like a diver's, pointing directly in the opposite.

"I think I know why this skeleton is lying in this odd way," observed Silver. "He's the compass."

We found out that the body pointed straight in the direction of the island, and the compass read duly E.S.E. and by E.

"I thought so!" cried the cook. "This is one of Flint's jokes. Flint had used one of his men as the compass. I know this is Allardyce."

"Come, come," continued Silver. "Now move ahead. We still have not found the treasure."

We started once again in the hot sun. The pirates no longer ran separate. They were all quiet and walked side by side.

After a while the whole party sat down. Silver took out his compass and checked for the directions.

"There are three 'tall trees'," he said. "Well, we are almost there. It's child's play to find the stuff now."

It was then, all of a sudden, out of the middle of the trees, a thin, high, trembling voice reached our ears,

"Fifteen men on the dead man's chest,
Yo-ho-ho and a bottle of rum!"

I had never thought that the pirates would be so scared. They turned pale and clung to each other.

"It's FLINT!" cried Merry.

The song had stopped as suddenly as it had begun, as if someone had laid his hand upon the singer's mouth. "Come," said Silver, struggling with his ashy lips to get a word out, "it's not a spirit. I know that. It has to be someone as alive as us."

"Darby M'Graw!" once again the voice wailed. "Darby M' Graw! Darby M' Graw!" Again and again and again and then rising a little higher, "Fetch the rum, Darby!"

The pirates remained rooted to the ground. It looked as if their eyes would pop out of their head. Long after the voice had died away, they still stared in silence, dreadfully, at each other. "That's it!" gasped one. "Let's go."

"These were HIS last words," moaned Morgan, "his last words."

Dick had his Bible out and was praying.

I could hear Silver's teeth rattle, but he had not yet given in.

"Friends!" he cried. "I am here to capture the treasure and I am not afraid of any spirit or living being. But there's one thing that is not clear to me. There was an echo. Now, no man has ever seen a spirit with a shadow or an echo. Well then, what's he doing with an echo to his voice?"

This argument seemed weak enough to me, but some of the men agreed with this.

Silver seemed lost in thoughts for a moment and then he cried out, "Ben Gunn!"

"Yes, it is Ben Gunn!" cried Morgan, springing on his knees. "Ben Gunn it is!"

"Why, dead or alive, Ben Gunn is not worth being afraid of!" exclaimed George Merry.

Once they were sure it was nobody else but Ben Gunn, their courage returned and they picked up their tools and set off again.

Dick, alone, still held his Bible and looked around him furtively, but he found no sympathy and even Silver made fun of him.

But as we walked on, Dick was growing sick. His fever was rising, as predicted by the doctor. Soon, we began to walk down the hill. We soon reached a tree that we thought was the first tall tree. But we were wrong.

The same thing happened with the second.

Soon, we saw a third one at a distance. It was nearly two hundred feet high. We knew it was the ONE, beneath which, seven hundred thousand pounds in gold lay buried!

The joy of finding this treasure made the pirates forget all their fears and they began to rush towards the tree.

Silver hobbled on his crutch, grunting all the while. In his excitement he had forgotten everything, even his promise to the doctor. I was sure that all he wanted was to seize the treasure, board the Hispaniola, under the cover of night, cut every honest throat about that island and sail away with the riches!

This realization made me tremble with fear. Soon, it became difficult for me to keep up with the pace of the treasure-hunters. Now and again I stumbled and it was then that Silver pulled, so roughly, at the rope and gave me his murderous glances.

We were now almost near the outer end of the wood. A low cry arose. Silver doubled his pace, digging away with the foot of his crutch and the next moment he came to a dead halt and so did I.

Before us was a great excavation. It was clear that it was not very recent. All was clear, the store had been found. THE SEVEN HUNDRED THOUSAND POUNDS WERE GONE!

Chapter 20

Fall of the Captain

ll of us were too shocked to say anything. But Silver recovered immediately from it and changed his plans before the others had time to realize what to do next.

"Jim," he whispered, "take this and be prepared for trouble."

Passing me a double-barreled pistol, he swiftly began moving northward. I could not help but whisper to him, "So you've changed sides again!"

Meanwhile, the pirates leaped at one another and began to dig with their fingers! Morgan found a two-guinea piece and it was circulated for quarter of a minute.

"Two guineas!" roared Merry, shaking it at Silver. "That's your seven hundred thousand pounds, is it? Friends, I tell you now that Captain Silver knew it all along. It is written all over his face."

"Ah, Merry," remarked Silver, "so you are trying to be the captain once again!"

But this time, everyone was entirely on Merry's side. They came out of the pit and stood on the opposite side of Silver.

And there we stood, two on one side, a boy and a one-legged man and five on the other with the pit between us. Silver did not move. He watched the others, coolly.

"Friends," Merry said, "they are just two. So let us …"

He was raising his arm and his voice to charge at us, when, Crack! Crack! Crack!

Three musket-shots flashed out of the thicket.

Merry fell dead into the excavation. The man with the bandage spun round, like a spinning top, and was dead. The other three turned and ran for their lives, with all their might.

Long John had fired two shots before Merry had the chance to create any mischief. At the same moment, the doctor, Gray and Ben Gunn joined us with smoking muskets.

"Forward!" cried the doctor. "Run quick, my boys. We must not let them take the boats."

We set off at a great pace. Silver had a lot of difficulty in keeping up with us. Leaping on his crutch, till the muscles of his chest were fit to burst, was something no one else could have done. As we reached the edge of the slope, Silver called out, "Doctor, see there! No need to hurry!"

Sure enough, there was no hurry. We could see the three survivors still running in the same direction they had started for. We were already between them and the boats and so we sat down to breathe.

As we walked downhill to the boats, the doctor related briefly what had taken place. Ben Gunn, the foolish maroon, was the hero from the very beginning.

Ben, in his long, lonely wanderings about the island had found the skeleton. It was he who had found the treasure. He had dug it up and carried it on his back. It took him a lot of time from the foot of the tall pine to his cave. He had stored the treasure in safety for the past two months, before the arrival of the Hispaniola.

The doctor came to know of this secret on the afternoon of the attack. The next morning, when he saw that the Hispaniola was not there in her anchorage, he went back to Long John and gave him the map, which was now quite useless. He gave him the food too, as Ben Gunn's cave was well supplied with goats' meat salted by himself.

"As for you, Jim," the doctor said, "it went against my heart, but since you did not stand by your duty, I did not have any option left but to leave you."

That morning, finding that I was in danger, the doctor had run all the way to the cave. Once there, he left the squire to guard the captain and took Gray and Ben Gunn to the treasure site. Soon, however, he saw that our party was ahead of him. Instantly, he remembered the superstitious beliefs of the pirates and that is how we heard Ben Gunn's voice.

"Ah," said Silver, "it was fortunate for me that I had Hawkins here. Had it not been for him, I would have been cut to pieces by them."

"Undoubtedly," replied Dr. Livesey, cheerfully.

By this time we had reached the boats. The doctor demolished one of them, and then we all got aboard the other and set out for North Inlet.

As we passed the two-pointed hill, we could see the mouth of Ben Gunn's cave and a figure standing by it. He was guarding with a musket. It was the squire. We waved a handkerchief and gave him three cheers. Silver joined us heartily.

The Hispaniola was there, cruising by herself, just as I had left her with the wrecked sail.

Soon, we got another sail ready and pulled round again to Rum Cove, the nearest point to Ben Gunn's cave. Once we were ashore, Gray returned, with the boat, to the Hispaniola, to guard the ship at night.

A gentle slope ran up from the beach to the entrance of the cave. At the top, the squire met us. He was cordial and kind to me as before and he did not mention about my running away, even once.

Silver politely saluted him.

"John Silver," said the squire, "although you're a prodigious villain, I will not prosecute you, as I am not supposed to."

"Thank-you, sir," Silver saluted again.

"Don't you dare thank me!" cried the squire. "Stand back!"

We all entered the cave. It was a large, airy place, with a little spring and a pool of clear water, overhung with ferns. The floor was full of sand. In front of a big fire lay Captain Smollett and in a far corner I saw great heaps of coins and bars of gold. Flint's treasure! This is what we had come for! This was what had cost the lives of seventeen men already! God knows how many ships were looted and how many countless men had been killed! The greed, shame and cruelty was incomparable!

"Come in, Jim," said the captain. "You're a good boy, Jim, but I don't think you and me will go to sea again. Is that you, John Silver? What brings you here, man?"

"Rejoining my duty, sir," replied Silver.

"Ah!" said the captain and that was all he said.

That night, saying a silent prayer for bringing my friends back to me, I enjoyed a great supper with all of them around me: Ben Gunn's salted goat, some delicacies and a bottle of old wine from the Hispaniola. Never, I am sure, were people gayer or happier. Silver was there in one corner, eating heartily, prompt to spring forward when anything was wanted. Once again he was the same bland, polite and submissive seaman of the beginning of the voyage.

Chapter 21

The Final Victory

he next day, early in the morning, we started transporting the huge load of treasure to the beach. The Hispaniola lay a few miles away.

Gray and Ben Gunn moved to and fro from the boat to the beach, loading, while the rest carried the treasure to the beach and piled it there. The men carried two bars at a time slung at the end of a rope, while I stayed there in the cave collecting the coins into large bags.

177

It was a pleasure sorting the strange collection, English, French, Spanish, Portuguese, Georges, and Louise's; and double guineas. Pictures of all the Kings of Europe, for the last hundred years, strange Oriental pieces, everything was there. By the end of it, my back ached with stooping and my fingers felt stiff.

This work went on for several days and we heard nothing of the three surviving mutineers.

After some time, I think it was on the third night, as the doctor and I strolled on the hill, we heard a faint murmur, which was difficult for us to understand.

"Heaven forgive them," said the doctor. "It is the mutineers!"

"All drunk, sir," Silver's voice came from behind us.

Well, that was the last news we had of the three pirates.

We decided to desert the pirates on the

island, instead of risking another mutiny by taking them aboard. We left them a good stock of powder and shot, the bulk of the salt goat, a few medicines, some tools, clothing, a spare sail and some ropes. Finally, one fine morning, we were ready to sail. And at last, to my inexpressible joy, the highest rock of Treasure Island had sunk into the blue sea.

Short of men on board, we all, except the captain, had to lend a hand. The captain, recovering and still in need of rest, gave his orders from his mattress. We headed for the nearest port in Spanish America and around sunset we anchored the Hispaniola. As soon as we reached the port, the shore boats full of Indians, selling fruits and vegetables, surrounded us.

I went to the shore along with the doctor and the squire to while away the early part of the night. Ben Gunn was on the deck alone. And when we came on board, Ben Gunn made a confession.

Silver was gone but not empty-handed. He had cut through a bulk, unobserved, and removed one of the sacks of coins, worth perhaps three or four hundred guineas, to help him on his further wanderings.

However, I think we were all pleased to be rid of him so cheaply.

Well, to cut a long story short, we hired a few people on board to help with the sailing and finally, the Hispaniola reached Bristol.

All of us had a generous share of the treasure and used it wisely or foolishly, according to our natures. Captain Smollett is now retired. Gray saved his money and is now mate and part owner of a fine ship. Besides, he is married and has a family. Ben Gunn got a thousand pounds, which he spent or lost in nineteen days and was back to begging on the twentieth. He was then given a lodge to keep and went on to become a great favorite among the country boys, as well as a notable singer in church on Sundays and Saints' days.

As for Silver, the man with one leg, who haunted me for a long time; no more was heard of him and he was finally out of my life. I hope wherever he is, he is living comfortably in the company of Captain Flint.

And I have lived my life comfortably ever since I returned home. But I still have the nightmares, sometimes dreaming of the huge ocean waves, raging about the coasts, or waking up in the middle of the night with the sharp voice of Captain Flint still ringing in my ears: "Pieces of eight! Pieces of eight!"

THE END